This book belongs to

_____

The Jungle Bop

By Nadia Mulara

for my
little monkeys

There's a monkey in the Jungle.

His name is Jungle Pants.

When he hears some music
he loves to have a dance.

He has a hippo friend,
Bubble Bottom is his name.

He and Jungle Pants like to play a little game.

When Bubble Bottom is full of wind that's when the fun begins...

Along came Sissy Strides who rattles with Bubble Bottoms sounds,

Then comes **Tommy Trumps**
and with his trunk he toots,

While Jungle Pants Continues
to Wiggle in his boots.

The Sleepy Lion

R-O-A-R-S

They all came to a ...

Stop!

But they will all come back tomorrow...

To have another Bop!

Can you name the
animals you saw?

Can you spot the
rhyming words?

Printed in Great Britain
by Amazon